Pete the Cat

I Love My White Shoes

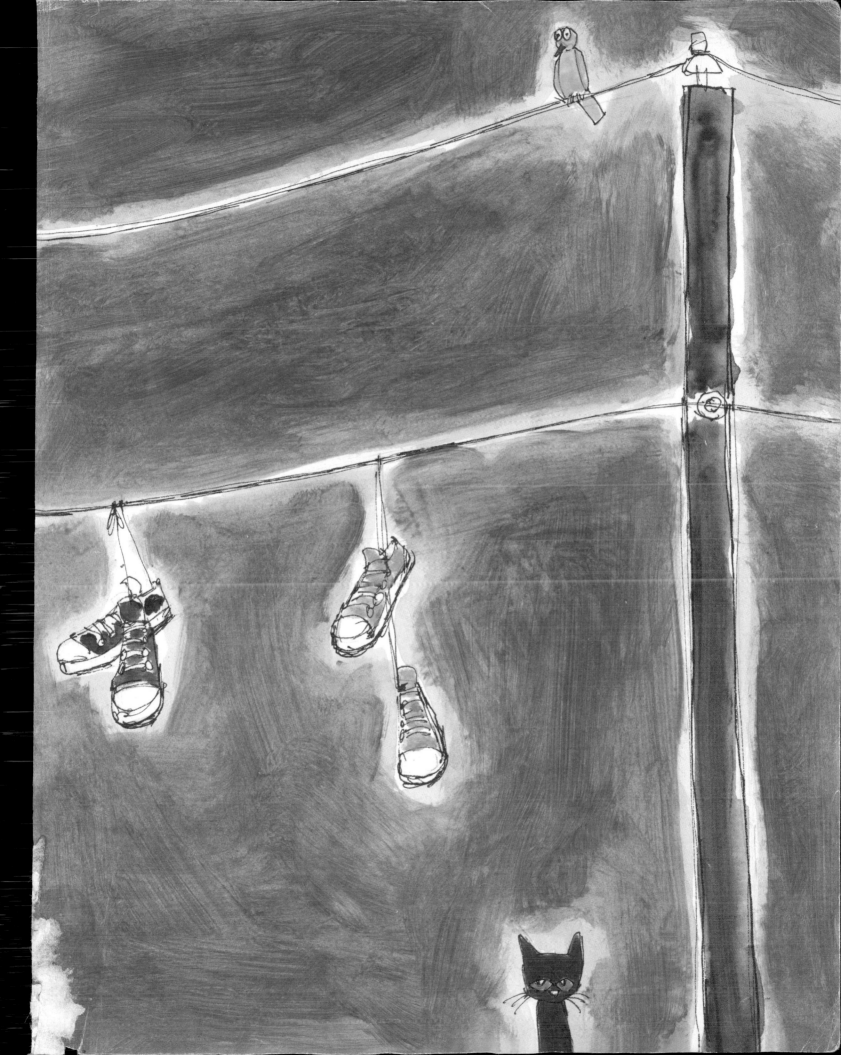

Pete the Cat

I Love My White Shoes

Story by Eric Litwin (aka Mr. Eric)

Art by James Dean

SCHOLASTIC INC.
New York Toronto London Auckland
Sydney Mexico City New Delhi Hong Kong

Pete the Cat was walking down the street in his brand-new white shoes. Pete loved his white shoes so much, he sang this song:

"I love my white shoes,

I love my white shoes,

I love my white shoes."

Oh no!

Pete stepped in a
large pile of ......

strawberries!

What color did it turn his shoes?

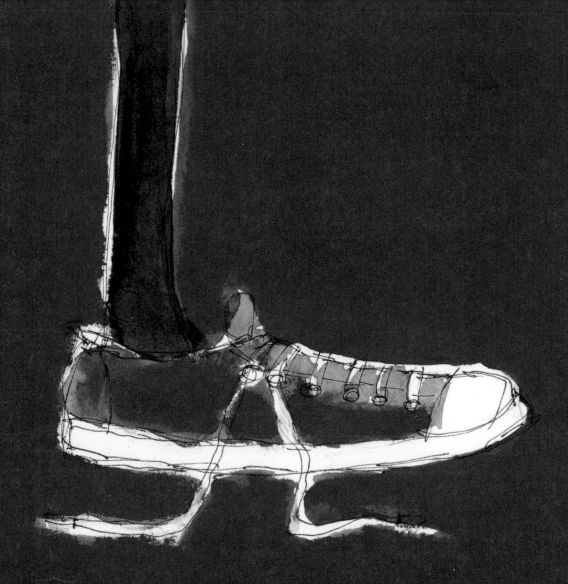

RED

Oh no!

Pete stepped in a
large pile of ......

"I love my
red shoes,
I love my
red shoes,
I love my
red shoes."

Did Pete cry?
Goodness, no!

He kept walking along and singing his song.

mud!

What color did it turn his shoes?

BROWN

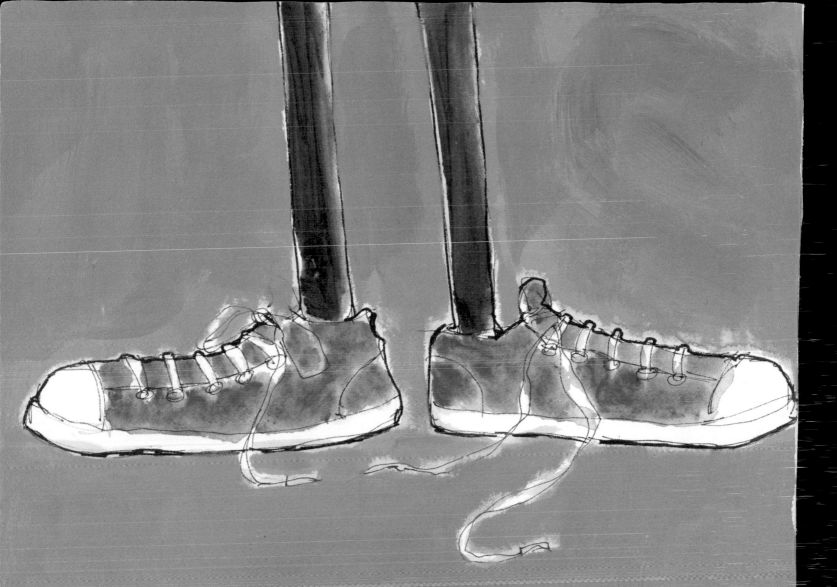

BLUE

blueberries!

What color did it turn his shoes?

Did Pete cry?
Goodness, no!

He kept walking along and singing his song.

"I love my blue shoes,
I love my
blue shoes,
I love my
blue shoes." ♫

Did Pete cry?
Goodness, no!

He kept walking along and singing his song.

"I love my
brown shoes,
I love my
brown shoes,
I love my
brown shoes." ♩♩

Oh no! Pete stepped in a bucket of water......

and all the brown,
and all the blue,
and all the red
were washed away.

What color were
his shoes again?

WHITE

But now they were WET.

Did Pete cry?
Goodness, no!

He kept walking along and singing his song.

"I love my WET shoes,

I love my WET shoes,

I love my WET shoes."

because it's all good.

This book began as a simple dream of Eric and James's.
Then the dream began to grow with help from some very
exceptional people. We are grateful to: Elizabeth Dulemba for
artist direction; Michael Levine for music production;
Marla Zafft for book design; Bobby Slotkin for legal counsel;
Karin Wilson from Page and Palette Bookstore
for sharing our book with HarperCollins.

ISBN 978-0-545-41966-6

12 11 10 9 8 7 6 5 4 3   11 12 13 14 15 16/0

Printed in the U.S.A.   08

First Scholastic printing, October 2011

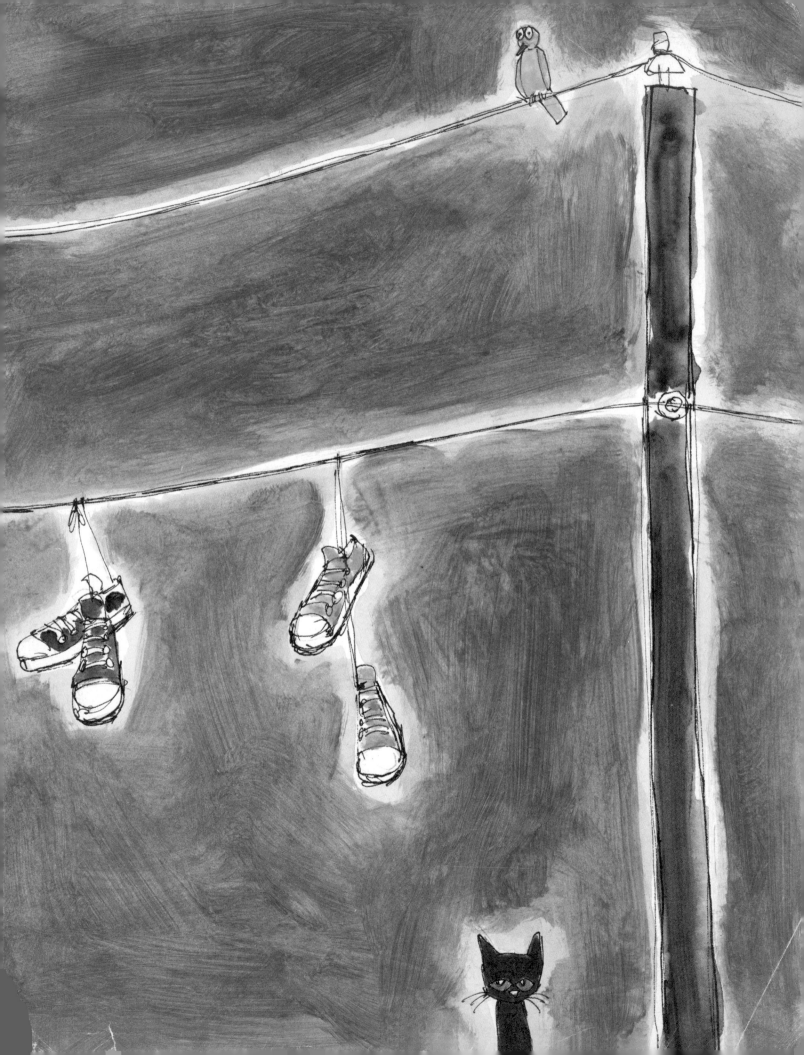